LO'

Hawaiian Style

SUSAN HORSNELL

USA Today Bestselling Author

Contents:

Copyright 4

Warning 5

Disclaimer 5

Chapter One 7

Chapter Two 18

Chapter Three 33

Chapter Four 46

Chapter Five 59

Chapter Six 74

Chapter Seven 87

Chapter Eight 98

About the Author 106

No 1 Best Sellers in 2018:

Matt – Book 1 in The Carter Brothers Series

Clay – Book 3 in The Carter Brothers Series

No 1 Best Seller in February 2019

Andrew's Outback Love – Book 1 in The Outback Australia Series

No 1 Best Seller in July 2019

Ruby's Outback Love – Book 2 in The Outback Australia Series

No 1 Best Seller in May 2019

Eight Letters

Best Seller in April 2020

Cora: Bride of South Dakota

LOVE, HAWAIIAN STYLE

Copyright © 2018 by Susan Horsnell

The right of Susan Horsnell to be identified as the author of this work has been asserted by her under the Copyright Amendment (Moral Rights) Act 2000

This is a work of fiction. Similarities to real people, places, or events are entirely coincidental.

Edited: Redline Editing
Proofread: Leanne Rogers
Published by: Lipstick Publishing
ABN: 573-575-99847

Warning

This book contains sexual content and language suitable only for those 18+

Disclaimer

This book is a work of fiction. Any resemblance to persons, living or dead, or places, events or locales is purely coincidental or historical. The characters are productions of the author's imagination and/or are used fictitiously.

Polena pa'a 'ia iho ke aloha i kuleana like ai kaua.

(In love tightly bound, you and I share equal rights.)

Chapter One

Corporal Lono Kapule groaned as the radio crackled to life and the dispatcher's voice reverberated over the airways. He had been looking forward to dropping the police vehicle back at the station and heading home. He had plans for a third-anniversary celebration. Soft candlelight, a lobster and seafood dinner, good champagne, and a night of fabulous fucking. Now his plans were shot to shit.

"Did you hear any of that Lono? You looked like you were miles away." His new Junior Officer partner, Anuhea Miller - known as Ana, asked. She had recently moved to the city, having previously been posted to a station on the North Shore. It was only their second shift together as members of Task Force *Lonoi*.

Task Force *Lonoi* consisted of a Senior and Junior Detective, a Corporal and three Junior Officers. They were pulled from normal duties to investigate, and hopefully solve, murder or any other capital crime which occurred in the Islands. Lono's previous partner had moved on to study Law. Ana was his replacement.

Lono cringed, he had been miles away. "Sorry, I was thinking about something else."

"Hikers have found a body. It's caught up on rocks on the beach side of the Diamond Head crater near the Beach Park. We've been ordered there. Detectives are enroute."

Lono flipped a switch, the siren and flashing lights burst into life. He checked the traffic and swung the vehicle around before speeding down Kalalaua Road towards Diamond Head.

"Lēʻahi," he corrected.

"Pardon?"

"That's what the locals call Diamond Head. Lēʻahi. The name is Hawaiian for tuna's dorsal fin. They insisted that was what the crater looked like."

"So why does everyone else call it Diamond Head?"

"British Sailors named it Diamond Head a few centuries ago. They thought the quartz they saw from their ships, which was flashing in the sunlight, was a diamond and the name was born. It stuck, but locals with a long history on Oahu only ever call it Le'ahi."

Lono slowed as they neared Honolulu Zoo. An elderly man and his wife tottered across the road. As soon as they had passed safely, his foot jammed down on the accelerator.

As they merged onto Beach Road, a large crowd captured their attention. People stood peering over the edge of the volcanic, rocky crags.

"I'd guess that's where the body is," Ana said.

Lono pulled the vehicle onto the shoulder of the road and screeched to a stop. "Radio the station. Tell them we need crowd control. The area will have to be cordoned off. The Detectives will hit the roof if they arrive and find their crime scene contaminated by onlookers. The last thing we need is for someone to slip and join whoever it is down there."

Ana reached for the radio on her shoulder, pressed the button and relayed her new boss's instructions to the dispatcher.

Lono stepped from the car, checked his Glock semi- automatic pistol was secure in his holster, and strode to the center of the milling crowd. He turned, his back to where the side of the crater dropped into the ocean. "Folks, I need you to move way back. Unless you have information about what has happened here, I would like you to return to your vehicles or homes."

The people in the crowd muttered and groaned but gradually dispersed, leaving only one couple behind.

"We found the body, Officer." A young man, who Lono estimated was in his mid-twenties, and a young woman around the same age, stood before him. It was clear they were shaken and he assumed they were the couple who had phoned the crime in.

Ana joined her partner, pen and notebook in hand. Lono excused himself to check on the victim while Ana spoke with the young couple.

"I walked to the edge so Dylan could take a photo with the water behind me. We're on our honeymoon and were taking a walk before dinner," the young woman began. "I saw something red and leaned over to take a closer look. That's when I saw her. Dylan phoned you straight away and no-one has been down there."

"Good. Did you see anyone in the area?" Ana asked.

Dylan and his new wife glanced at each other. "No, there was no-one close by. When Marilyn screamed, people came rushing from all directions."

Ana scribbled in her notebook. "If you think of anything at all, please call the station." She wrote down their names and contact numbers before allowing them to leave. She made her way to where Lono crouched, peering over the edge.

She squatted beside him. The body was that of a young woman. The red top she had been wearing was in tatters and her golden breasts were exposed as she lay, trapped in the rocks. A large black mole was visible on her right shoulder. Water gently lapped over her. Whatever she'd been wearing on the bottom half of her body was gone.

"She hasn't been here long," Lono said. He pointed down and Ana followed the line of his hand. "Her skin is only slightly puckered which indicates she hasn't been here long. She doesn't look burnt either, yet she is fully exposed to the sun."

A car screeched to a stop behind them, the two officers swung around. It was the task force Detectives. Within seconds, two more police cars arrived and the Coroner's Office vehicle. An ambulance brought up the rear.

Lono and Ana approached the Detectives who climbed from their car.

"Officer's," the deep honeyed voice greeted.

Lono pulled Ana closer. "Ana, this is Senior Detective Atoni Kinimaka and his partner Detective Roger Kamaka. This is Junior Officer, Anuhea Miller. Ana, as she likes to be known, has just been transferred to our task force from the North Shore station."

The Detectives shook hands with the shapely young police officer.

Ana raked her eyes over her superiors. The one called Kamaka wore a wedding ring so he was off limits. The other, however, had no such encumbrance. He was tall, Lono and she would have been hard pressed to meet this goliath's shoulders. His chest was broad and she imagined he was well put together. His waist was slim as were his hips. Those legs went on forever. She licked her lips. *His cock must be enormous.*

When she finally tore her eyes from the handsome stud's body, she noticed the look passing between him and her partner. She could barely suppress her groan of disappointment. *Why are the gorgeous ones gay?*

Atoni dragged his eyes from the love of his life and glanced at the young officer standing alongside. She was petite. Her hair was jet black like most Hawaiians and her black eyed gaze was now firmly fixed on him. Had she guessed? She certainly had a knowing expression. His lips curled into a smile.

He knows I suspect. Ana gazed into eyes so brown they were closer to black. His hair was a curly, unruly mass and his skin, the golden color of all native Hawaiians. *The man is perfect. Fucking perfect. Again, why is he gay?*

Lono cleared his throat and Ana swung around to face him. His thickened cock caught her eye. He wasn't hard but, there...it definitely flinched. *Yep, I'm out of luck with these two. Not that Lono is my type. He's handsome alright, with his unblemished golden skin, thick glossy brown hair, trimmed short around his ears but he's way too short. He must only be three or four inches taller than me. Bod's not bad though.* She glanced back at Atoni. *These two must work out, and not only in bed.*

The man from the Coroner's Office interrupted her lustful thoughts as he stepped closer. "Detectives. What have you found?"

Atoni answered. "We've only just arrived, Mike. I'll let the Officers give you the initial report."

Lono gave the Detectives and Coroner a report of what he'd observed as they moved to where the victim lay.

The five men peered over the edge. Unfortunately, the water was rising over the young woman.

"Better get down there while we can. It won't be long before that tide comes in and the water will be too deep to find anything. I'll get some rope." Mike started towards his vehicle.

"Bring a couple of those officer's back with you. The cordon can wait," Atoni barked.

~*~

Mike was lowered over the edge first to assess the body. Atoni followed close behind. There was a small platform near where the body lay, the two burly men barely fit on it. As Mike checked the victim, Atoni searched the area for clues.

Something sparkling in the sun, off to the side, caught Atoni's eye and he negotiated the rocks to move closer. Donning rubber gloves, he bent down and picked up the object. He scouted the immediate area but found nothing further. He stood and moved closer to Mike.

"How did she die?" Atoni asked.

"There are ligature marks on her neck and dark bruising, she's been strangled. Strange pattern though. I haven't seen it before."

Atoni held the shell lei close for Mike to observe. "Could this be the murder weapon?"

Mike studied the lei made from small brown and white conch shells. The shells are most likely threaded on fishing line. He glanced back at the woman's neck. "Pretty sure that's what was used, but I'll be able to give you a definite answer when I get her back to the lab."

"How long do you reckon she's been dead?"

Mike dragged his fingers through his hair. "No more than an hour."

"Why the hell didn't anyone see anything?"

"Don't ask me. I only get to tell you what happened."

Atoni lowered his voice. "Has she been violated?"

"Not sure but my guess would be yes." He held the lips of her pussy apart.

Atoni could clearly see small tears and bruising on the sensitive skin. "So we're looking for someone who likes to rape and kill?"

"Yep. She fought hard too. Look at the bruising on her forearms and her broken nails." He held her arms in the air.

"With any luck you'll find some skin under her nails and we might be able to get some DNA from it."

The clear aquamarine water lapped at their feet. The tide was rising fast.

"We better get her out while we still can. I've got everything I need," Mike stood up.

Atoni signaled to the men and women waiting above. "Send down a stretcher."

The gurney from the ambulance was lowered over the edge, down to the men. Atoni steadied it and both him and Mike stepped back to lower it onto the small platform. It hung over the edge but it was all the room the men had. It would have to do.

Atoni lifted the victim from her watery grave and placed her onto the stretcher. He covered her body with a sheet, taken from the stretcher, and secured her with ropes. "Haul her up. Take it slow," he instructed.

He watched with Mike as the stretcher was maneuvered back to the top and disappeared out of sight. The police lowered ropes and they both scrambled up the cliff side to join their colleagues.

Atoni brushed off his suit pants as he watched the paramedics close the doors of the ambulance before climbing inside and driving away.

"I'll give you a call as soon as I have some information." Mike slapped Atoni's shoulder before ambling back to his vehicle.

"Found anything Kamaka?" Atoni asked. "Where have Kapule and his partner gone?" He was disappointed to find Lono was no longer there.

"I sent them door to door in the area to see if we can find out who the deceased was and if anyone noticed anything." Kamaka answered. "The others will finish cordoning off the area and then do a thorough search."

"Looks like it's gonna be a late night." Atoni had been looking forward to a quiet evening at home to celebrate his and Lono's third anniversary. He had been preoccupied with thoughts of his lover laying across his knees, he would spank his ass until it turned red. Relaxing in the Jacuzzi with a glass of fine wine and then tying Lono to the bed so he could fuck him until he screamed and begged for release. He suppressed a groan of frustration.

"What's wrong, Boss?" Kamaka asked.

"Nothing. Let's get this over with so we can at least get some time at home tonight."

The Detectives scoured the area searching for a clue that, with any luck, would lead them to the killer.

Chapter Two

The Detectives and Officers had scoured the area where the young woman had been found. Apart from a few flattened bushes and broken branches, there was nothing.

Police, with a description in hand, had been door knocking the immediate area for almost three hours. Nobody seemed to know the lovely girl. Atoni and his partner were convinced she was a local, not a tourist. Something in their 'guts' insisted she was from the surrounding area. So far, their gut feelings, weren't proving correct.

Atoni glanced up when Roger placed a hot coffee on the desk in front of him.

"Any luck, Boss?"

"Nothing. I told the officers to go home. It's getting too late to disturb people. They can try again tomorrow."

"Maybe we're wrong. Maybe the victim was a tourist."

Atoni appeared thoughtful. "My gut tells me she's local but if nothing turns up tomorrow, we'll start checking hotels for missing tourists."

"I'd have thought someone local would have reported her missing by now. It's almost five hours since she was found and it's splashed all over the news."

"I don't understand it either. Why don't you go home? There's nothing else we can do now, we'll start again in the morning."

"What about you?"

"I'll finish off this initial report of the scene and then call it a night."

"Okay. I'll see you tomorrow. At the scene or here?"

"Can Jenny drop you off at the scene?"

"Yeah. She can swing past on her way to taking the kids to school."

"I'll bring the squad car and meet you there."

Roger neatly stacked the papers on his desk, gathered his car keys and strode from the office.

Atoni was alone. He sighed as he gulped a mouthful of coffee. Lono would be waiting for him at their apartment and he was desperate to join him. He scribbled the last few sentences hurriedly, flicked off his desk lamp and sprinted from the building. It was almost nine o'clock – plenty of time left for what he had planned.

~*~

Atoni switched off the engine and climbed from his car. He'd swung past the late-night florist and picked up a huge bunch of yellow hibiscus flowers – Lono's favorites. Turning the key in the lock, he pushed the door open and stepped into the foyer of their apartment.

Lono greeted him and Atoni pulled him into his arms. Lowering his head, he captured his lips in a deep, sensuous kiss.

"I've been waiting for you," Lono was breathless when they drew apart.

Atoni handed his lover the bouquet as he ran his fingers through Lono's hair. "I came home as soon as I could. Happy Anniversary, sweetheart."

"Oooh, my favorite. They're gorgeous, darling. Thank you and, Happy Anniversary to you too. I can't believe it's been three years." Lono stood on tiptoe and planted a kiss on Atoni's cheek. "I have dinner ready."

With Atoni's arm around Lono's waist, they moved into the living area. Soft light flickered from dozens of candles. *Lono is such a romantic,* he thought.

"I'll put these in water while you freshen up. Don't be long, I'll miss you."

"Are you giving me orders?" A wicked glint lit up Atoni's eyes.

"Of course not, darling. I know I would pay for doing that. I'm only suggesting."

"It didn't sound that way to me. Maybe I'll have to punish you later. Maybe, since it's our anniversary, I'll forgive you."

Lono's dick danced in his pants. He couldn't wait for dinner to be over so they could retire to their bedroom. He knew Atoni would have something special planned.

Lono watched the rise and fall of Atoni's ass as he headed for their bedroom to change.

Lono was setting the last of the seafood platters on the table when Atoni returned.

"Is that all of it, sweetheart?" Atoni asked.

"Yes. Your timing is perfect."

Atoni pulled out a chair and Lono sat down. A tender kiss captured his lips as his napkin was unfolded and placed on his lap. "Thank you, darling."

Atoni sat and unfolded his napkin while he perused the decadent selection of seafood laid out before him. "This looks wonderful, sweetheart." He helped himself to lobster and oysters. The platters were handed to Lono, who stacked his plate.

The first oyster slid down Lono's throat before he spoke. "Hell of a day. Any luck with finding out who the girl was?"

"Not yet. I'm convinced she's a local although Roger isn't so sure anymore. He thinks someone would have reported her missing before now."

"It's strange, no-one seems to know her. I thought if she was local, someone would have recognized the description we gave out. It doesn't make sense."

"Yeah, that has me baffled too. Here on the island, everyone knows everyone within a six block radius."

"Maybe she's a new arrival and the neighbors haven't met her yet?"

Atoni broke off a lobster claw and sucked the white meat into his mouth before licking his lips. "Maybe. Hopefully tomorrow will turn something up."

"How's the dinner?"

"Delicious, as usual. You have missed your calling, sweetheart. You should have been a chef. This seafood sauce is heavenly. Did you make it as usual?"

Lono smiled. "Of course, darling. Only the freshest ingredients grace our table and you don't get that from a jar or a bottle."

Atoni chuckled. "You spoil me. I have to work out twice as hard these days. If I didn't I would be an overweight porky and you would leave me for someone trim, taut and terrific. I don't know how you maintain such a luscious body, you hardly ever work out."

"I would never leave you, you own my heart and, I get enough of a workout in our bedroom."

Atoni chuckled again. "Hurry up and finish eating. I have been thinking about fucking you all day and I can't hold out much longer."

Lono placed the lobster claw he'd been wrestling with onto his plate and rinsed his fingers in the bowl of water alongside him. "I'm finished but what about dessert?"

"Did you get the strawberries and cream I asked you for?"

"Yes, I did and I made the gooey, chocolate sauce you wanted too."

Atoni smiled. "We're ready then."

Lono stared at his gorgeous partner as they both stood. "I don't understand. Do you want dessert after we fuck?"

Atoni held his hand out and Lono placed his hand in it. "Come with me. You will understand soon."

They moved to the bedroom where the giant, king-sized bed took pride of place. The bedhead and foot were intricately carved. It had been a prized piece of furniture, handed down to Atoni by his Grandfather. The two men loved it. Lono ensured it was kept in peak condition by lovingly oiling the wood on a regular basis.

The lovers faced each other and fingers reached for each other's shirts. As they slipped each button from the holes holding them captive, muscled chests were revealed.

Atoni slipped the shirt from Lono's shoulders as he nipped and kissed at his neck.

Lono trembled. His fingers refused to function and undo the last of Atoni buttons. Shivers of lust danced through his body, his cock stood to attention.

Atoni sucked a nipple into his mouth and bit gently while he unfastened the belt holding Lono's shorts on his hips.

Lono groaned as he held Atoni's head to first one nipple, then the other. He had given up on attempting to remove his lover's shirt. He was completely lost in a world of euphoria.

"Atoni, I love you so desperately, my darling. Please, I need you, now."

Atoni dropped to his knees and slipped Lono's shorts and underpants from his body, leaving him naked. For a man of average height, he was hung like a Texas longhorn. The aroused cock stood proud before him, droplets of arousal sparkled on the tip. He reached out and gathered the throbbing rod into his mouth, his hands cupped the globes of Lono's ass and held firm.

"Honey, please. My legs are beginning to buckle."

Atoni stood and swept Lono into his arms, turning to the side, he laid him on the bed. He took the opportunity to strip. His cock's hardness matched his lover's.

The mattress sank as Atoni crawled towards a now squirming Lono.

Their lips locked and, as their kiss deepened, their hands frantically fondled each other's bodies.

Lono thrust his hips towards Atoni. Their cocks flinched and twitched. The feeling for both men was deliciously erotic but both needed more.

"Roll over," Atoni growled with desire.

As Lono did as he was asked, Atoni sheathed his rod.

"Hold the headboard and get up on your knees."

Lono had barely obeyed before he was slammed against the bed head by the ferocity of Atoni's dick invading his asshole. He cried out with joy and pushed his backside back against his lover. Tingles swept through him, his cock ached for more.

"Darling, may I use my hands?" Lono wanted to jack himself off, he needed release.

"No, you may not. You will have pleasure only from me tonight. Do not ask again."

Lono knew better than to groan with frustration. There had been many a night where he had protested and Atoni had left him tied up and suffering. He remained quiet but cooperative while Atoni fucked himself to release.

Stars burst in front of Atoni's eyes as he held Lono's hips and thrust hard one more time. Semen erupted from his cock, filling the latex covering, and giving him the relief he had been seeking all day. Now the ache was relieved he could play. He withdrew his cock, padded to the bathroom and disposed of the condom.

"Roll onto your back," he ordered and Lono flipped himself over.

Atoni reached into his nightstand and withdrew black, silk scarves. Lono's cock jumped with excitement. It was his turn – at least he hoped it was.

One look from his sated partner told Lono to spread his legs and lift his arms. He was quickly secured to the bed, his mouth was bound and a blindfold tied in place. Then, to his distress, Atoni left the room.

He wriggled frantically. *No, no, no! Not tonight.*

When he heard Atoni come back into their room he sighed with relief. Something was placed down on the nightstand.

Lono shook with excitement. What was Atoni doing?

"Did you think I had left you sweetheart?" Lono nodded and Atoni chuckled. "Not tonight my love. I have other more pleasurable ways for you to suffer tonight."

He sat on the side of the bed and reached for the icy cold carton of ice cream. Using a spoon, he dropped a large glob onto the head of Lono's erect dick.

Lono tried to scream. What the fuck was happening? The cold was intense, his dick shriveled.

Atoni smiled as the dick shrank into itself. "Oh dear, are you suddenly not aroused by me? That will not do." Lifting the now flaccid cock, he dropped another large glob onto the balls.

Lono writhed frantically. The pain from the cold was unbearable. His dick and his balls were trying to climb up inside his belly. He wanted to be untied and have a hot bath, it would allow his man parts to recover.

Atoni chuckled. "You don't like dessert, sweetheart? It seems I will have to eat it alone." He lowered his head and licked away the icy cold fare.

Lono's cock hardened. The cold of a few moments ago, all but forgotten. His ass wiggled, his hips lifted. He was feeling good again.

Atoni sucked the thickening dick into his mouth, laved the tip and pushed his tongue into the slit. Once more it was steel hard and awaiting release. *Not for a while yet, lover.*

He reached for the bowl of hot, gooey chocolate and tested it with his finger. He wanted to cause pain but not damage. The chocolate was hot but not scalding. On a dick it would feel so much hotter than it actually was. Lono was going to suffer excruciating pain, just the way he often told Atoni he liked it.

"I see you are randy again. Do you want to be fucked?"

Lono nodded his head frantically.

"Not yet, my sweetheart. I haven't finished dessert."

Shit, fuck, what now. Lono tried to spin onto his side. He wanted to take his dick out of Atoni's reach.

"Ah, ah, ah. You know I will not be denied." Atoni ladled hot chocolate sauce onto the tip of Lono's cock, some disappeared down the slit.

Lono's muffled cries could be heard, in spite of his binding. He breathed rapidly and Atoni watched him carefully. He knew not to push him too far.

Shit, I'm on fire. The pain, such delicious pain, what the fuck is he doing to me? He pulled against his restraints despite knowing he would never be able to get free. Slowly the burning subsided and he began to relax. His cock lay soft, shrunken against his belly.

As the hot liquid hit his cock again and ran down his balls, it was almost more than he could endure. Tears ran from his blindfolded eyes. He bucked like an unbroken stallion as the liquid burned a path on its travels. Cries erupted from the depths of his chest but came out as muffled whimpers. Lono was confident, despite the pain, Atoni would never push him past his limit.

Atoni watched sweat pour from Lono's body. He had outdone himself this time. His lover was feeling intense pain, just how he liked it. The pleasure of finally coming, would be so much more pleasurable for his adored lover—when Atoni allowed it.

Lono collapsed back onto the bed as the burning finally subsided. *No more, please no more.* His begging was not to be heard.

"Hmmm, did you enjoy that? What can we try next?"

Lono shook his head violently to convey he'd had enough.

"You don't know? Well, I'll have to think of something." Atoni smiled as he removed the ice cream and chocolate soaked towel from under Lono's ass before replacing it with a clean one.

Atoni padded from the room to reheat the chocolate sauce and remove the rest of the ice cream from the freezer.

Lono relaxed. He was alone, he could recover. He wanted to sleep. He began drifting off.

When Atoni returned, he noticed the slow, steady, rise and fall of Lono's chest. He had fallen asleep. That wouldn't do. He gathered the soft dick into his hands and fondled it. In a matter of moments, Lono was fully awake and his dick stood tall.

Atoni held the excited rod with one hand and dolloped icy cold cream over the head.

Lono bucked. His cock protested violently.

Chocolate sauce was poured over, the cream melted instantly and the combination flowed over the cock and Atoni's hand. The combination continued, icy cold, hot.

Lono silently begged as sweat poured from his body. Tears soaked his blindfold and his body bucked and twisted. Finally, it stopped. He waited, not sure what Atoni now had in mind. His cock was still being held captive in the big man's hand.

"And, now..."

Lono clenched his ass, his body stiffened.

"Me." Atoni lowered his mouth over the chocolate and melted ice cream covered cock. He licked the full length of one side, then the other before taking the head into his mouth and swirling his tongue over the tip. He probed into the slit, suckled and laved.

Lono's hips bucked, pushing his cock further into Atoni's mouth. His body was on fire, alive. The pressure built steadily. His cock pulsed.

Atoni had the cock buried to the hilt and as he pleasured it with his tongue, it began pulsing and throbbing. It was only a matter of seconds before his lover exploded.

Lono almost blacked out with the sheer force of his climax. Semen pumped from his cock and flowed down Atoni's throat. The flicking tongue continued to work him, drawing every spasm of orgasmic pleasure from him. It seemed to go on forever but finally he began to slowly descend.

It was over. Atoni had finished. Lono could relax and recover.

Atoni released the traumatized, but now satisfied dick, and padded off to the bathroom. He flicked the taps on the spa and poured in a soothing combination of oils. He returned to the bed, released Lono from his bindings and gathered him into his arms.

Lono sobbed into his chest as Atoni kissed the top of his head. "Happy Anniversary, lover. Did I please you?"

"Atoni, I have never felt such excruciating pain and such a powerful climax. It was better than anything I have ever experienced before. Thank you. I will never forget this Anniversary."

Atoni captured his lips. Their tongues danced, twisted and twirled. They were so much in love. The intensity of their feelings transcended anything either of them had ever known.

Chapter Three

Lono groaned when Atoni's pager buzzed loudly. He had only just dropped off to sleep after they had spent half the night pleasuring each other's bodies. He snuggled closer into Atoni's chest and draped one arm over his shoulder.

Atoni checked the pager and picked up his mobile phone. It was four o'clock in the morning. He dialed the station number. The night Sargent's voice boomed down the line. "Sargent Mason."

"Senior Detective Atoni, I was paged."

"Yes, Sir. I have a couple here at the station who are reporting their niece missing. I thought you should know."

"Did they say where they live?"

"Yes, Sir. Kaalawai Place."

"That's off Diamond Head Road near where the girl was found." Atoni sat up causing Lono's head to slam back on the pillow. "I'll be right there." He disconnected the call.

"What's going on, darling?" Lono sat up.

Atoni stood and pulled on his pants before sitting back on the bed and slipping his shoes on. "There's a couple at the station who say their niece is missing. They live just a couple of blocks from where we found the murder victim."

"Do you want me to come with you?"

"No sweetheart. Get some sleep and I'll catch up with you later." He leaned over and gently kissed Lono's lips. "I love you."

"I love you too. Be careful."

Lono watched as his lover left the room before rolling over and drifting back to sleep.

~*~

The police station carpark housed only three vehicles. It was very different from during the day when it was constantly full. Atoni pulled into a spot near the entry doors and switched off the motor. He exited his vehicle and pressed a button on his remote. The car beeped and lights flashed indicating everything was now locked.

He pushed through the foyer doors and strode to the front desk.

"Detective Atoni?" The desk Sargent asked when he saw him approaching.

The man was young, Atoni had never seen him before. *Must be a transfer.* "Yes. Mason wasn't it?"

"Yes, Sir."

Atoni saw the young man's eyes indicate a couple sitting to his right. They were middle-aged, appeared to be Hawaiian – the golden skin color and raven black hair usually gave the natives away – and they clung to each other's hands for dear life. Atoni approached them with his hand outstretched.

"Senior Detective Atoni. I believe you are reporting your niece missing?"

He shook hands with the man when he stood. "Yes, we are. Nohea was supposed to be staying overnight with a friend. We called the house about an hour ago to let her know Leialoha was sick but her friend said she had never arrived. She thought our niece had changed her mind about going there. We checked with her other friends and no-one has heard from her." He took a shuddering breath. "We heard about the murdered girl and when we couldn't find Nohea, my wife and I panicked."

"Come through to my office and we'll talk. Would you like coffee?" Atoni offered.

"I would like tea please," the woman said in a tremulous voice.

"Nothing for me, thank you," her husband replied.

"How do you have your tea?" Atoni enquired.

"Just cream please."

"Sargent, could you please get the lady a cup of tea. I'll have a black coffee while you're at it."

"Certainly, Sir. I'll bring them to your office." The Sargent disappeared to the kitchen.

Atoni led the distraught couple through to his office. He flicked a switch on the wall which turned on the lights and offered them chairs in front of his desk.

They were all seated when Mason brought in two steaming mugs and placed them down on the desk. "Will that be all, Sir?"

"That will be all. Thank you, Sargent."

He vacated the room and closed the door with a soft click.

Atoni lifted his mug and sipped at his scalding hot coffee. After placing it back on his desk, he picked up his pen. "First of all, can you tell me your names and your niece's name?"

"I'm Aukai Okamu and this is my wife Ka Pua. Our niece is called Nohea Okamu."

Atoni wrote the names down. "Who is Leialoha? You said she was sick?"

"Yes, she has a tummy upset. We have left her with a neighbor. He's a doctor so will keep a close eye on her. She is Nohea's three-year-old daughter." The husband was doing the talking. His wife obviously too distressed to contribute to the conversation.

"Why is Nohea with you? Is she visiting?"

"No, she moved here about a month ago from the Big Island. Her parents, my brother and his wife, were killed in a boating accident and she had no-one else. We offered to take her and Leialoha in until they could get back on their feet."

That would explain why no-one in the area knew the victim. "What about her husband, partner? The father of her child? Brothers, sisters?"

"The father didn't want anything to do with her or the child so she had been living with her parents until they were killed. She's an only child."

Atoni scribbled the information onto his pad. "Can you give me a description of Nohea and what she was wearing?"

The woman spoke up. "My husband was at work when she left. She was wearing a red shirt, white skirt and white sandals." She began sobbing. Her husband wrapped his arm around her and held her close.

"She's about five feet three inches tall, waist length, black hair and dark brown eyes. She has a large mole on her right shoulder. She's twenty-four years old."

Atoni struggled not to cringe. They had the identity of their victim. Now came the worst, fucking part of the job — telling the relatives. "Mr. and Mrs. Okamu, I'm sorry ..."

"NO!" The woman jumped to her feet and screamed.

Her husband attempted to calm her but, she was hysterical with grief. Her screaming was deafening. Atoni made a quick phone call although he was barely able to hear above the din.

He stood and rounded his desk. He gently placed his hand on her shoulder. "Mrs. Okamu, I have a doctor coming to give you something to help you through your grief. I'm so sorry for your loss."

Tears rolled down Mr. Okamu cheeks as he tried to deal with his own grief and calm his wife.

Atoni dragged his fingers through his hair. The couple had sunk to the floor and, gripping each other tightly, they rocked back and forth. Mrs. Okamu's eyes were glazed over, she was now almost catatonic. *I'll find the bastard who has caused this family unspeakable grief and, when I do, I'll make sure he rots in jail.*

Atoni's thoughts were interrupted by a light tap on the door. He hurried to open it. The Police doctor stood facing him and he ushered him into his office.

"This couple have just been informed, their niece is our murder victim. I'm worried about Mrs. Okamu. She was screaming for a few minutes but now she appears to be in deep shock."

"I'll take care of them," the doctor said.

"I'll go and call the morgue to see if I can bring Mr. Okamu down to formally identify the body. I don't know if he's up to it but it has to be done."

"I'll take Mrs. Okamu to the lounge and give her a sedative. By the time you have made your call, Mr. Okamu should be ready to go with you."

"Thank you," Atoni said as he left the office.

~*~

Atoni stood alongside Mr. Okamu as the morgue attendant pulled open a drawer to reveal the girl. "Oh, dear God. That's her."

Atoni reached out to steady the grief-stricken man before leading him into an adjoining room where he could sit down.

Mr. Okamu flopped into a chair, dropped his head into his hands and sobbed. His body shook violently as he cried.

Atoni felt helpless. He hated being in this position. He wanted to kill the bastard who had murdered this man's niece. "Can I get you a coffee?"

Mr. Okamu lifted his head. "Why? Why did they kill her? She never hurt anyone. She was trying to give her child a good upbringing." He paused for a moment, wiped his eyes and blew his nose. "What the hell are we going to tell Nohea? How do we tell a three-year-old, she no longer has a mummy?"

Atoni placed his hand on Mr. Okamu's shoulder. "I'm so very sorry. We will do whatever we can to find whoever did this."

"Thank you. If you don't mind, I'd like to take my wife home."

"Of course." Atoni led the distressed man back to the lounge where his wife now sat quietly.

As the Detective and her husband returned to the lounge, Mrs. Okamu lifted her eyes. Atoni noticed the smallest nod of the head from her husband.

"Nooooo," she screamed. Mr. Okamu gathered his wife into his arms.

"Please take as much time as you need. If you don't mind, my partner and I will come by tomorrow and ask you a few more questions."

"That'll be fine," Mr. Okamu answered.

"If you think of anything unusual that has happened in the past few days, give me a call." Atoni placed his card on the coffee table in front of the couple.

He returned to his office. It was going to be a long day. He badly wanted to catch the killer and so far he didn't have one fucking clue.

Atoni was pouring over the notes from the crime scene when Roger strode in.

"Morning, Boss." He placed a hot coffee on the desk in front of his partner before pulling up a chair.

"Jenny obviously gave you the message to come in instead of going out to the scene. I hope it wasn't any trouble for her."

"None at all. What's going on?"

"We have the identity of our victim. The night Sargent called me at four this morning to say he had a couple reporting their niece missing. The murder victim turned out to be her."

"Did they have any idea who might have killed her?"

"None at all, but they were pretty upset."

"Who was she?" Roger asked.

"Nohea Okamu. Twenty-four years old, single mother. Daughter, Leialoha is three years old. No other living relatives. Nohea's parents were killed in a boating accident off the Big Island about a month ago and she moved in with her aunt and uncle. The father of the little girl has had no contact."

"Why was she out so late?"

"She wasn't. She was supposed to be staying overnight with a friend. Her daughter became ill and the aunt tried to call to let her know. That's when they found out she had never made it to her friend's home."

"Have they identified the body?"

"Mr. Okamu gave us a positive ID."

"That must have been hard."

"Yeah. They're both devastated. We have to find the asshole who did this."

"We will. Any leads yet?"

"Nothing. Fucking nothing."

The two detectives sipped their coffee. Both were lost in thought when Corporal Lono Kapule knocked gently on the office door.

"Come," Atoni ordered.

Lono entered with a smile but, one look at the stress on his lover's face caused him to frown. He hated seeing Atoni under pressure. He wanted to rush over and fold him into his arms, reassure him everything would be okay. But, they weren't alone.

"Yes, Kapule. Do you need me?"

Oh yes, I need you. "Sarg asked if you wanted everyone at the briefing this morning or just the Task Force?" Lono answered.

Atoni noted the smoldering desire in his lover's eyes. He wanted to leap from his chair and pull Lono into his arms. His cock hardened, hidden by the desk, thank the Lord. Up to now, they had managed to keep their relationship a secret from others on the Police force. All hell would break loose if word got out. The police motto, *Integrity, Respect and Fairness*, would be thrown to the wolves.

"I have a few things to clear up before we leave the station. I'll be at my desk when you're ready to leave." Roger left the office, closing the door with a click. Did he suspect?

Lono turned the key in the lock and rushed to Atoni's side. "What's happened, darling?" He pulled Atoni out of his chair and into his arms.

"We have an identity on the murder victim. She was a single mom. She was living with her Aunt and Uncle, her parents were killed less than a month ago. Her little girl is only three years old. You'll hear the rest at the briefing. I want the whole task force at the scene. We have to find something."

"My God, three years old and, to lose her mother in such horrifying circumstances, one week before Christmas."

"I know. It's a tragedy for the families no matter what time of year they lose a loved one but, to happen so close to Christmas......" Atoni shook his head, fighting back anger.

"I'll organize something for the little girl. Is the family well off?"

"Average, I guess. Not paupers but certainly not wealthy."

"I'll take up a collection to buy Christmas presents for all of them and maybe we could start a trust fund. Her Aunt and Uncle could put the money towards her education.

Atoni lowered his lips onto Lono's and kissed him seductively before pulling away. "You're always so thoughtful, sweetheart."

"I better get to the briefing room before someone comes looking for us. Oh, do you want all of us or the task force?"

"Only the task force." Atoni answered.

Lono nodded as he unlocked the door before slipping away. Both men hated having to be so secretive and furtive about their relationship.

Chapter Four

Lono placed his coffee on his desk and flopped into his chair with a thud.

"Problem?" Ana asked.

He dragged his fingers through his hair. "The victim has been identified. Young mother with a three-year-old kid. I'm gonna organize a collection for Christmas presents and hopefully get an Education fund started."

"Good idea." Ana reached into her purse and pulled out a one-hundred-dollar bill. She held it towards her partner. "This will get you started."

Lono raised an eyebrow. One hundred dollars was a great deal of money for any cop but especially a junior officer.

"I get an allowance from my parents. They're very well off, the allowance is generous," she said in answer to his questioning stare.

He took the money. "I'll have to get a few boxes or jars to keep the money in. We can leave them at different places in the station. One at the front desk, one out the back with the Detectives and one in here."

"That's a good idea. I noticed you came in from the Detectives area. Were you speaking with someone in particular?"

Lono knew his partner was fishing. She had a mischievous, knowing twinkle in her eyes. "Yeah, I was down there talking to a couple of them about yesterday's murder." *Not exactly a lie*.

Ana nodded her head but Lono had a sickening feeling, she was on to them. Why was it always the women who picked up on things? For three years they had managed to keep the men at the station in the dark and had avoided getting too close to the women. Having a female for a partner, were things about to change? Was their world about to come crashing down around them? He had too much on his mind to worry about it now.

He stood up from his desk. "I'm going back to the kitchen to get rid of this mug. I'll see you in the briefing room."

Ana watched her partner stride away. *Hmmm, strange. If he has nothing to hide, why did he run from me like I had the plague?*

The briefing went as Lono had expected. Atoni told the Officers what he had already told him and filled in a few details.

"I want everyone in Task Force Lonoi out at the site today. I want every stone turned, every blade of grass scrutinized. We have a murderer out there and I want him found. The dog squad will be there with two dogs. I want every inch of Lē'ahi combed for clues. I want this asshole found before Christmas. I want to give this family closure, understood?"

The officers mumbled their agreement and nodded their heads.

Lono found himself becoming aroused. He adored forceful, serious, Atoni.

"That's it for now. Detective Kamaka and I will be on site today. If you find anything at all, report it to one of us immediately. Dismissed."

Chairs scraped the floor as the officers stood before exiting the room. The slightest of glances passed between Atoni and Lono. Love was in their eyes. It went unseen by everyone — except Ana.

Oh yeah. I'm onto their relationship. I wonder if everyone knows and keeps it quiet, or, if I'm the only one who suspects? Ana decided to discreetly fish for information from her fellow police officers at some time during the day.

~*~

Two police officers, along with the two detectives, scoured the area where Nohea had been found. Two other police officers were door knocking, asking questions. The dog squad would arrive later in the day.

Atoni's back and legs ached. It was hard for such a big man to be bent over for hours on end but he was going to check every inch of the site even if it killed him.

Lono ambled over to where the detectives were searching. "Sir." He winced when he noticed the pain lining Atoni's face as he straightened.

"Yes, Corporal. Have you found something?" Roger asked hopefully.

"Not a damn thing. I thought it might be a good idea to break for lunch."

Atoni checked his watch. It was after one thirty, they had been searching since eight. No wonder his back and legs were killing him. "Good idea. How about we slip down to the hotel for something? With any luck we might pick up some gossip."

"Do you want to take both cars, Sir?" Lono asked.

"No, we'll all go in ours." Roger answered.

Lono called Ana over and explained what they were doing. She slid into the back seat of the car with her partner, Roger sat in the passenger front seat and Atoni slipped behind the wheel.

"Too hot, my back is killing me and my legs are numb. I could use about four Mai Tai's," Ana grumbled.

Atoni glared at her courtesy of the rear vision mirror.

Ana caught the glare. "Don't get your balls knotted, Boss. Pineapple Iced Tea will do just fine while I'm on duty." Her tone, as well as the words, were derogatory.

Atoni stiffened. Lono's head snapped around to his partner in disbelief. Juniors *never* disrespected their superiors, not if they wanted to have a career.

Atoni spoke in a low voice, his tone menacing. "I do *not* get my balls knotted and I will thank you to show respect when you speak to your senior officers. If you intend to remain as a member of this task force you would do well to learn respect very fast. Trying to track down clues is tedious, difficult and time-consuming. It affects all of us and it is not an excuse for poor behavior. Until the murderer is located, there will be no consumption of alcohol at all. Is that clear?"

"What! Not even after hours?" Ana persisted.

Atoni's knuckles turned white as he gripped the steering wheel, frustration with the junior officer was building. Ana's background report had hit his desk two weeks before she had been assigned to the task force. He had read she came from a very wealthy, North Shore family. As an only child she had been educated at the best boarding schools on the mainland and given everything her heart desired. Her references had been excellent; they were the reason he had signed off on her joining. He was beginning to have second thoughts. "One glass of wine, or a beer, is the absolute limit during the investigation. There is no *after hours* during this time."

"That's not real fair. What if the investigation takes months?"

"You can always ask to be reassigned," Atoni said.

Lono's cock danced with excitement as the exchange continued. He loved it when Atoni became frustrated or angry. How he wished they were at home where he would have experienced the release of that frustration.

Atoni pulled into the hotel carpark, exited the car, threw the keys at Roger and stomped into the building.

"He's not real happy with you, young lady. If you want to keep your position on this task force, you will do well to heed his warning about showing respect," Roger said.

"You have to remember you are only a junior officer with a lot to learn, Ana. If you mind your manners, you could learn a great deal from Detective Atoni." Lono added.

"I'll apologize later," she conceded as they made their way into the hotel.

~*~

Atoni was seated on a bar stool waiting for the bartender to finish preparing an iced tea. The scowl on his face made it plain, he was not happy.

"There's a table over there," Ana said as she threaded her way through other full tables. The lunchtime crowd were still in attendance.

"I'll get drinks. Iced tea?" Lono asked.

Roger nodded.

"Pineapple for me," Ana shouted over the noise.

Lono stepped up next to Atoni and ordered the drinks. "I'm sorry, love. I meant to warn you, Ana can be a bit rude," he whispered while he waited for the order to be filled.

The bartender slid Atoni's drink towards him. He lifted it to his lips and took a large gulp before turning towards Lono. "She's going to be difficult to work with if she doesn't lose the attitude. Not all of us are as sweet and easygoing as you."

"I know she pushes your buttons. I promise I'll try and straighten her out but we have a bigger problem."

Atoni raised his eyebrows.

"I think she has worked out we're in a relationship."

"How the fuck did she work that out?" Atoni glanced towards the table where Ana was deep in conversation with Roger.

"I have no idea. You know I can't figure women out."

"How do you know then?"

"Trust me darling, she knows."

"Detective Kamaka, can I ask you a question?" Anna began.

"Of course, you can. That's how junior police officers learn."

Ana swallowed hard. "How long have Detective Atoni and Officer Kapule been in a relationship?" She giggled when Roger's eyes almost bugged out of his head. "You didn't know?"

"I had no fucking idea and Atoni's been my partner for almost two years. Now you mention it, he never talks about women. Shit, he's never even talked about being on a date. That would explain it."

"Do you think anyone else at the station knows?"

"Not as far as I know. There would have been a reaction from some of the macho officers if they knew. Fuck - Lono and Atoni, gay. Thinking about it, I guess there have been a few subtle signs."

"How do you feel about it?"

Roger narrowed his eyes. "Doesn't make a scrap of fucking difference to me. Atoni's a bloody good Detective. He's kind, helpful and taught me almost everything I know about conducting criminal investigations. I hope you're not thinking of causing problems for them."

"Of course not. It's a shame the good looking ones have to be that way inclined though." She turned towards the bar. Atoni's eyes were fixed on her. Had Lono voiced his suspicions about her discovering their secret? She winked mischievously.

Atoni's eyes hadn't left Ana. When she turned towards him and winked, he knew Lono was right. "Fuck. Do you think she'll talk?"

"Count on it. I have a feeling she could be quite the troublemaker."

Atoni groaned as he turned back to the bar and took another gulp of his drink. He wished he had forgone his own rules and laced it with alcohol. "I have a sinking feeling; our careers could be about to go up in flames."

"Don't jump to conclusions yet. Captain Alepeleke is a fair man. Do you think we should talk to him before she has a chance to cause chaos?"

"Hmm, I don't know. Let me give it some thought first." Atoni watched as the three drinks Lono had ordered were placed in front of him.

The men gathered the drinks and pushed their way to the table. The waitress sauntered over as they were seated and they each gave their orders.

"Detective Kinimaka, Sir."

Atoni's shoulders tensed. "Yes, officer."

"I'm sorry about earlier. I was out of line and I apologize. Sometimes I let my attitude run away from me, I have a lot of growing up to do. It won't happen again."

"Oh, it will Ana. But, there are ways to question my decisions without being rude."

Lono smiled as he sipped his tea. His man was such a sweetie. Yeah, he loved to put forward a tough, no-nonsense exterior but, Lono knew he was a softie at heart. He cared deeply about people, especially those he works with.

"You don't mind me asking you questions even if they're about the decisions you make?"

"Not at all. That's how junior police officers learn. The more questions you are willing to ask, the better you will become at your job."

"Thank you, Sir." Ana glanced at Roger. Atoni had validated what he had already told her.

The waitress returned and slid plates of food onto the table. She stood nervously clenching and unclenching her hands and Atoni guessed she had something to say.

"Do you have something you need to say..." Atoni checked the girls name tag, "....Molly?"

"Sir. It's about the girl you found murdered yesterday. I think I might have seen her arguing with someone when I was going home after my shift."

Lono stood and pulled up an extra chair next to Atoni. "Sit down. I'll go and let the bartender know we're questioning you."

Molly sat while Atoni headed for the bar. Within moments he returned.

"He said to take as long as you need."

Molly was relieved. She needed this job and didn't want to irritate her boss.

"Now, you think you saw something yesterday?" Atoni asked. He would be the one to do the questioning but all four police members had paper and pens at the ready to write everything down.

"Yes. I was going past the beach side of Lē'ahi when I saw a couple arguing. I saw one of them slap the other hard across the face."

"What time was this?"

"About three fifteen. I was on early shift and left at about ten to three."

"Was anyone else around?"

"I didn't see anyone. The couple disappeared towards the beach. The track has thick bush and lots of trees. You have to climb over rocks to get to the water and it's pretty steep. Hardly anyone uses it unless they want privacy to make out. I didn't think anything of it until I heard the news this morning."

"Was the girl wearing a red blouse?"

"One of them was. The other was wearing a green dress with a white flower print."

All eyes fastened on Molly.

"They were both females?" Atoni asked.

"Yes, they were."

"We've been looking for a fucking male. All this time wasted. We were going in the wrong direction. We need to talk with the family. Thank you, Molly. You have been a huge help."

Atoni pushed back his chair and stood. The other three followed suit. Lunch would have to wait. They followed their boss back to the car.

Chapter Five

Atoni dropped Lono and Ana back at the scene with instructions to check every inch of the beach track. He drove with Roger, to the home of the victim's aunt and uncle. Hopefully they could answer his questions.

The house was a cream painted concrete single story bungalow with beautifully manicured gardens and lawn. Atoni and Kamaka strode purposefully to the large stained oak front door. Atoni molded his hand into a fist and rapped twice.

Mr. Okamu swung the door open and looked anxiously at the Detectives.

Atoni noticed a small child grasping her uncle's leg and peering out from behind. She had the largest blue eyes he had ever seen on a child. It was unusual to see blue eyes on Hawaiians, usually they were either black or brown. Her jet black hair contrasted sharply with her pale ivory skin. *Her father must be a white man.*

"Sorry to disturb you, Sir but we have had some new information come to light and we would like to ask you a few questions. May we come in?" Atoni was the perfect gentleman.

Mr. Okamu reached down and swung the child into his arms before inviting the officers inside. He led them from the foyer into a living room and gestured for them to be seated.

The living room was immaculate, a wall of windows allowed the area to be flooded with sunlight. Two large, dark brown leather sofas were begging for backsides and a sturdy oak coffee table divided the two. "Can I get you coffee, cold drink?" their somewhat reluctant host, asked.

The detectives shook their heads and thanked him for the offer. Nothing was required. Atoni pulled out a notebook and pen while he waited for Mr. Okamu to be seated. He sat the child on his lap.

"I'm sorry I have to keep Leialoha with me, my wife has been sedated and is sleeping."

"We understand and won't say anything that she shouldn't hear," Atoni assured him.

"You mentioned your niece was supposed to be staying with a friend on the day she was murdered. Do you know who the friend is?"

"Her name is Olina Akahele. She lives with her family at Apartment 71, 49 Beach Road. Olina's father is the City Auditor. The girls met at the Palm Leaf Hotel, where Nohea had a part time job, and became friends pretty much straight away. They go out from time to time and Nohea has stayed at the apartment on a couple of occasions. We were nervous about Nohea walking through the isolated area near the crater."

"Had you ever seen or heard them arguing before?" Atoni asked.

"No, but Olina rarely came here. In the month Nohea had known her, I think she came here only twice."

"Do you know if she had any reason to harm your niece?" Atoni worded his questions carefully with the child in the room.

"None that I know of and, when I discussed this with my wife, she had no idea of anyone who might want to hurt her."

"My mummy's gone to Heaven. Auntie and Uncle are going to take care of me," the little girl blurted out.

Atoni's heart thudded in his chest. It seemed so unfair that this gorgeous little girl should now grow up without her mother. He was at a loss for words. He didn't miss the overwhelming sadness in Mr. Okamu's eyes. "I'm sorry," he whispered.

"Leialoha, go and see if Auntie is awake." Her uncle placed the little girl on the floor and they watched as she ran from the room. "We can talk plainly for a few moments. Do you suspect Olina of Nohea's murder? I thought the Coroner believed she'd been raped? I don't understand."

"We have a witness who saw two girls arguing before they headed up the beach track near where Nohea was found. We believe it was Olina and Nohea." Roger explained.

"But why? Why would Olina hurt Nohea and a girl couldn't have raped our niece?"

"We have no idea, it's the reason we came to you. We were hoping you could tell us," Atoni said.

"What will you do now?"

"We'll head to the Coroner's office and talk with Mike, the Coroner on the case. Maybe Olina led Nohea to a male waiting along the beach track. Maybe, and this is only speculation because I don't have facts, they both murdered your niece."

Atoni and Kamaka stood and offered their hands to the distraught man. They shook in turn.

"Will you keep me informed?"

"We will let you know as soon as we have something."

"Uncle, uncle. Auntie asked if she could have some water please." The little girl leaped at Mr. Okamu and he swept her into his arms.

"We'll see ourselves out. Thank you for your help," Atoni said as he turned.

"Bye, misters," the little girl called as they left.

Atoni closed the front door with a soft click and the two detectives strode to their car.

"She's the same age as Rosy. I can't imagine my kids having to grow up without a parent," Roger said as they both slid into the vehicle.

"I know. We're gonna find out who did this for that little girl and that's a promise."

Atoni fired up the engine and sped off towards the Coroner's office with more questions to ask.

~*~

"Mike," Atoni said as he stepped into the Coroner's office.

"Atoni, Roger, I left a message for you at the station. Close the door please and have a seat."

The two Detectives did as they were asked.

"There's something strange about your murder victim." Mike stated.

"In what way?" Atoni asked.

"Well, she died from strangulation which we pretty much knew, but, she wasn't raped. I don't understand it. You saw the scratches and bruises on her vagina but there was no penetration. The only possible explanation is, whoever did this was interrupted."

"Or the murderer is a woman trying to make it look like a man," Roger said.

Mike's eyes turned towards Roger. "A woman? Most unusual. What makes you think that?"

"We have a witness who saw two women arguing in the vicinity at the time the victim was murdered," Atoni said.

"The victim was small and slim so I suppose a larger woman could have the strength to overpower her."

"What about the skin under the fingernails?" Roger asked.

"The DNA isn't in the system so the murderer was clean until now."

"Anything else?" Atoni asked.

"Well, she has at some stage given birth to a child."

"She has a three-year-old daughter, Atoni said."

That's about it then. The body is being released for burial. The relatives have been notified."

The Detectives stood and Mike mirrored them on the other side of his desk. They shook hands before leaving.

~*~

Roger stood at Atoni's side and watched as he knocked at the Judge's office door.

"Come in," Judge Hie called out.

Atoni and Roger entered the office and stood behind a large, carved oak desk. The Judge glanced up and indicated for them to be seated before continuing to scribble notes on a pad. The detectives waited for him to finish.

The Judge placed his pen down and looked up. "Gentlemen, what can I do for you?"

"We're here to see about procuring a warrant, Sir," Atoni said.

"Tell me your reasons and make them good."

Roger explained the murder case they were working on.

"We require a warrant to test the DNA of Ms. Akahele, Sir. Skin taken from under the fingernails of the victim was tested but the DNA was found not to be in the system," Atoni added.

"You are sure this young woman is responsible for the victim's demise?" The Judge asked.

"We're as sure as we can be, Sir. We have a witness who came forward with a description of the girl who was seen with the deceased not long before her body was discovered."

"I will grant the warrant for a DNA sample to be taken. I will not give permission for the premises to be searched at this stage. If the DNA is a match, come back and I will grant you a search warrant at that time."

The Judge opened his desk drawer and pulled out a form which he began scribbling details on.

"Sir, I don't think a search of the premises will be required," Atoni said.

The Judge paused and glanced up.

"The murder weapon was a shell lei and it was found near the body at the scene. We have no reason to believe there is anything at the apartment which would be of use," Atoni continued.

"You think she would have dumped the clothing she was wearing?"

"Yes, I do, Sir. If the DNA is a match, the girl will have scratches visible and we can ask our witness to formally identify her. I believe it will give us a strong case."

"Well, it seems you have a very strong case and strong justification for the warrant. I need the name and address of your suspect. Does she live alone?" The Judge waited for the detectives to answer.

"The suspect is thought to reside at the address with her family, Sir." Roger advised after Atoni had given the Judge Olina's name and address.

"Sir, we also request permission to hold the suspect in custody, without charges, pending the DNA results," Atoni said.

"Why?"

"Sir, the suspect is from a wealthy family and we fear they may assist her to flee the islands." Atoni glanced at Roger for his agreement.

"The family lives in a waterfront apartment in a very prestigious suburb, Sir. They have the means and, we suspect the contacts, to assist their daughter with escape."

"Granted, but, only until the results come back. If the samples match – charge her, if not – let her go."

"Thank you, Sir."

The detectives thanked the Judge again as Atoni accepted the document. They left to bring Olina in to the station for testing and questioning.

~*~

Roger stood to the side, out of view, as Atoni rapped on the apartment door. A young woman in her early twenties greeted them. She was tall, muscular, probably worked out. She appeared to have the build to cause someone as small as Nohea, physical harm. The side of her face had several large scratches and there was another big scratch on her throat. Atoni was convinced, this was their murderer.

"Yes, can I help you?" She lifted her hand to cover the scratches.

"I'm Detective Kinimaka and this is my partner Detective Kamaka." Roger stepped from the shadows and the girl flinched. "Are you Olina Akahele?" Atoni continued.

"Yes," she answered warily.

"We'd like to ask you some questions about Nohea Okamu. May we come in?" Atoni asked.

The girl's death grip on the door was causing her knuckles to whiten. Atoni knew she was uncertain and nervous.

"There's no-one else here," she said. Her grip on the door remained tight.

"We only need to speak with you. We can take you down to the Police Station if you would feel more comfortable," Atoni said.

Her fingers loosened and she opened the door wide. The Detectives stepped inside the plush apartment.

"Come through to the living room, please?" Olina led the way and waited for the men to be seated before sitting herself.

Atoni would take the lead in the questioning. Roger would speak only when he felt something needed to be clarified. He would take notes and record the interview. He placed a recorder on the coffee table in front of him and flicked it on.

"We will be recording this interview, Miss Akahele," Atoni informed.

Olina nodded her head in understanding.

"I'm sorry miss but you must verbally state you understand this interview is being recorded."

"Sorry. Yes, I understand this interview is being recorded."

"Miss Akahele, when did you last see your friend, Miss Okamu?"

"We weren't friends. We met at the hotel where she works and went out a couple of times."

"Her family seems to be under the impression, you were good friends. She stayed here at this apartment on a few occasions, is that correct?"

Olina trembled. "Y..yes, but we weren't really friends."

"Alright, I'll accept that for now. When was the last time you saw or spoke with Miss Okamu?"

"I haven't seen, or talked with her, for days."

"You didn't see her on the day of her murder? She told her family, she was spending the night with you."

"No, I don't know anything about that. We never had plans for her to stay here on that night," she lied.

"When her uncle phoned your home in the early hours of the morning, why did you say Miss Okamu must have changed her mind about staying if that was never the intention and you knew nothing about it?"

"I..I don't know. I must have been sleepy and didn't realize what I was saying."

"Did you meet Miss Okamu near the beach track on the afternoon of her death?"

"No, I didn't."

"Do you own a green dress with a white flower print?"

"I don't know, why?"

"Would you be willing to check your closet?"

"I thought about it and I don't have one."

Atoni let it go but, maybe he would need a search warrant. It appeared she may not have disposed of the dress after all.

"Miss Akahele, I have to inform you -you are under arrest for the Murder of Miss Nohea Okamu." He Mirandized her and ensured she understood what was happening. "We have a witness who saw you wearing a green dress with a white flower print, on the afternoon Miss Okamu was murdered. The witness has said she saw two women arguing near the start of the beach track. One of the women slapped the other before they disappeared down the track."

The detectives noticed Olina slump in the chair.

"Why did you murder Miss Okamu?" Atoni asked softly. He was hoping she would answer but had already informed her, she had the right to remain silent.

Olina glanced at the detectives, a lone tear tracked a path down her cheek. The men noted the guilt in her eyes.

"I didn't mean to. I met her near the track so we could walk back here together. I was excited because I had arranged for us to go out with two men we met at the hotel. Nohea didn't like them. She insisted they were trouble and probably into drugs. She said if I persisted in seeing either of them, she would tell my family they were unsuitable."

Olina paused.

"I told her she was a snitch and slapped her. She took my hand and asked me to go with her so we could talk sensibly. She led me down the beach track to the ledge overlooking rocks. I tried talking to her but she wouldn't listen. Before I knew what I was doing, I took off my lei, wrapped it around her throat, and pulled it tight. I wanted to scare her so she wouldn't say anything."

"Are you saying, it wasn't your intention to kill her?" Atoni asked.

"No, of course not. I thought I would frighten her into keeping quiet so I could go out with the guys even if she didn't want to. I must have held the lei too tight for too long. She got blue around the lips. When I let go, she wasn't breathing. I tried to revive her, I breathed in her mouth, but she wouldn't breath."

"What did you do after that?"

"I panicked when I realized she was dead. I ripped her skirt and panties off and scratched up her pussy. I ripped her blouse and then pushed her off the ledge, onto the rocks."

"Why did you do that?" Roger spoke for the first time.

"I was scared. I wanted it to look like a man had attacked her. I didn't see anyone in the area and thought I would get away with it."

"Miss Akahele, please stand." Atoni had heard everything he needed to. He pulled her hands behind her back and snapped on the handcuffs.

Olina sobbed. "I'm sorry."

Atoni led her out to the car, leaving Roger to lock up the apartment. *Two young, fuckin' lives destroyed and over something as trivial as going out on a date.* Atoni hated to see young lives ruined needlessly.

Roger had no doubt Olina was sorry, but was she sorry she had murdered Nohea or, sorry she had been caught?

The men escorted their prisoner back to the station. It had been a long but productive day. Nohea's family would have their closure.

Chapter Six

Atoni turned his key in the lock of the apartment door and dragged himself inside. It had been a long and traumatic day.

"Lono, where are you?"

"Kitchen, darling."

Atoni kicked off his boots, threw his keys on the table in the hall, and hurried through to the kitchen.

Lono met him near the doorway, glass of red wine in his outstretched hand.

Atoni accepted the glass and leaned down to place a kiss on his lover's lips. "Mmmm, I needed that."

"I hear you got the girl who murdered Miss Okamu." Lono moved back to the stove and the stir fry he was preparing.

Atoni followed and peered into the pan. "Moroccan Chicken, yum. Yes we did. It was her so called friend and she confessed. I don't want to talk about it now. I want to spend time with you, have a quiet dinner and fuck your brains out."

"Oooh, sounds good to me. Supper will only be a few more minutes."

Atoni placed his glass on the bench. "I'll go and wash up." He strode from the room.

Lono's eyebrows shot up when Atoni returned. He was wearing a very short, tight pair of shorts and nothing else. His cock hardened at the sight before him. "Not your usual dinner attire, honey."

Atoni gave his partner a devilish smile. "No, does it turn you on?"

Lono approached his lover and ran his hands over his chest. "It's been three years and I still marvel at how I landed such a gorgeous man."

Their lips locked in a passionate and urgent kiss. When they drew apart, both sets of eyes smoldered.

"Supper can wait." Atoni's tone indicated, it was a demand, not a request.

Lono made the mistake of not realizing it.

Atoni did not like his demands to be ignored and Lono usually paid for doing so.

"Darling, it's ready and I can't guarantee it will keep," Lono protested. "I want to eat first." A mistake.

Atoni reached over Lono's shoulder and turned off the flame under the wok. He grasped his lover's hand and led him through to the bedroom.

Atoni sat on the bed and positioned Lono in front of him. "Strip." His face was as dark as a summer's day storm.

Lono quickly removed his clothes. His cock pointed skyward, he wanted the fuck every bit as much as Atoni did. "Are you angry, darling?"

"Did I tell you supper could wait?"

Shit. Lono realized he had protested against the demand. His cock danced as he stood, naked and exposed. His lover's eyes raking over him as his tongue moistened his lips. He lowered his eyes. "Yes, I'm sorry."

"For what?"

"For saying I wanted to do something else. Please Atoni, can't you forget it just this once?"

"Do you want me to?"

"Yes, please."

"Why?"

"Because we're both tired and I didn't think."

"So you think you can disobey me and not be punished because you're tired?"

Lono lowered his head. His cock was so hard it ached. "I guess not. What would you like, darling?"

Atoni thought for a moment. "*Black Cat*. When you begin answering back, it is obvious, I have been treating you too softly."

It took all Lono's willpower not to groan. *Black Cat*, a rubber flogger, with numerous long, tails caused more pain than all the other floggers and paddles combined. He stepped to the cupboard, withdrew the flogger and handed it to Atoni. He stood waiting for instructions.

"The wheel, I think." Atoni stood and led the way into the spare room.

Hooks were positioned in the walls and the ceiling, there were benches of varying heights and an old set of wooden stocks. Although Lono noted the equipment, it was the huge iron wheel in the center of the room, he stepped up to.

Atoni strapped his lover's legs and arms firmly in place. Lono was now spread eagled and at Atoni's mercy. A gag was fixed firmly in place, screaming, begging and pleading, would be useless.

Atoni stroked the flogger down Lono's back, over his rounded ass, and down his legs. He shivered as the rubber teased numerous nerve endings. His cock was ready to burst. When a hand locked over his rod, he thought he would explode. His knees buckled putting weight on his arms.

"Your cock is powerful hard, my love. You want to come, you need to come," Atoni whispered in his ear as he fondled his dick.

Lono's dick pulsated, drops of cum sparkled on the tip. His ass tightened and flexed. If only Atoni would close his fist around the throbbing appendage and bring him relief. He was so close. Then – nothing, the hand was gone. Lono glanced down, his cock was blue, filled with blood, ready to detonate.

Laughter came from behind him. "You didn't really think I was going to let you come first did you? You will come when I say you can and not before."

Lono groaned with frustration. Why wouldn't his cock stop pulsing and dancing? It was agony. When the flogger connected with his ass, he shouted in shock, not that it was heard. *Sonofabitch!* He jiggled his ass, attempting to relieve some of the sting.

Again, the flogger bit into his skin. Thank fuck, he wasn't working tomorrow. He was going to be deliciously sore. When tendrils flicked between his legs and connected with his balls, he roared. This was the reason, he had a love/hate relationship with the floggers. Not only did your ass suffer, but your dick and your balls.

His cock softened, but was still hard enough with want to ache. The ache changed with the next flick of the flogger. Tendrils connected with both his balls and his dick. His cock shrank instantly, trying to withdraw into his body. It was almost as though it was trying to hide. Tears streamed from his eyes.

Five more lashes, his ass was on fire, his balls numb and his cock shriveled.

Atoni appeared before him. He wiped at the tears. "Enough?"

Lono nodded ever so slightly. His lover pretended not to notice.

"No? You want more?" He moved back behind him and lashed him again.

After four more lashes, Lono thrashed. As much as he delighted in having pain inflicted on him, he'd had enough. Atoni stood before him.

"I can't give any more, sweetheart. Your ass is bright red. I'm worried your skin will break. I have to stop whether you want me to or not." He untied Lono who collapsed into his arms.

He made his way to the bedroom and lay his wounded lover on the bed. "I'll run a bath. I'm not sure I should allow you to take such punishment sweetheart."

Lono's eyes widened. "But, I love the pain. It makes me happy and it helps you to get out your frustration."

Atoni brushed hair off Lono's forehead. "My sick, twisted love. I will continue to give you the pain you desire but I have to draw the line at injuring you. You are not going to be able to sit on your ass for at least two days. It's lucky you're off duty." He kissed Lono's lips before making his way to their bathroom. He flicked on the taps, adjusted the heat and added soothing oils. It was going to hurt like hell when the water hit Lono's reddened ass.

~*~

Lono sat on two cushions as he forked chicken into his mouth. Atoni had given him two Advil for the pain but his ass throbbed like hell. It felt wonderful.

"I think you'll be giving me a head job tonight. It's not a good idea for me to be ramming my hips into your sore ass," Atoni said.

Lono sipped at his wine. His cock was rising. "I can manage you fucking me but if you prefer me sucking you off, I'm happy with that too."

"Hmm, I think you will mouth fuck me and then, you can hand fuck me while you bring your cock to satisfaction in my ass."

Both men's rods now resembled steel. Arousal was building.

Lono smiled. "Sounds good, darling."

"Hurry up and eat so we can get on with it."

Lono obeyed by forking more food into his mouth.

When Atoni stood to place his dishes into the dishwasher, Lono followed. Once the washer was loaded, they held hands and headed to their bedroom.

Atoni lay on his back, his cock at attention. Lono crawled onto the bed and plunged the stiffened rod into darkness. As his tongue fondled and teased, his teeth scraped and nipped. Atoni groaned with pleasure. His dick commenced dancing.

Lono tasted droplets of the sweet nectar of love. He cupped the expectant balls, squeezing and stroking.

Atoni's hips gyrated. His hands held Lono's head in place. His fingers seemed to be everywhere, tweaking and twisting nipples, raking over his chest, dragging up his legs. The man was like a fucking octopus. His cock pulsed. Darkness peppered his vision as he flew into space, then, with one huge suck from Lono, he erupted. Stars burst before his eyes, nectar flowed from his tip. The climax was eked out, until Atoni was sure he couldn't take any more.

Slowly, carefully, Lono brought him back down to earth. Atoni was spent, his body trembled with satisfaction. His breathing heavy and ragged. He dragged Lono into his arms. "I love you so much." He peppered his face with kisses.

Lono wrapped his hand around Atoni's cock and squeezed. It leaped back to life and squirmed beneath the firm touch.

Atoni rolled onto his side. Lono positioned his dick and eased into the ass. It was like heaven as the muscles swallowed him up and tightened around him.

He pumped in and out, his cock swelling, hardening. His hands began coaxing Atoni towards Climax as he kissed his shoulder and murmured into his ear. "Your cock is hard as steel, I can feel your desire in your balls. They're tense, ready to spill. Come with me, darling."

With a roar, Atoni again emptied his sacs. Lono exploded within. Their bodies writhed, both cocks pulsed with pleasure. Then – quiet. Both men were exhausted. Atoni rolled towards

Lono and they kissed passionately before dropping into a satisfied slumber.

~*~

The sound of the shower brought Lono out of his slumber and he rolled onto his back to stretch. He leaped from the bed. "Fucking hell," he roared.

Atoni appeared from the shower within seconds. Dripping wet and naked, he rushed toward Lono and snatched him into his arms. "What the fuck happened?"

"I rolled onto my ass and it felt like a million hot needles were piercing it." Tears dripped off his chin as he snuggled his head into Atoni's chest.

Atoni felt guilty, had he gone too far? He ran his hand over Lono's back. "I'm sorry darling. I should have stopped sooner."

"It felt so good at the time." Lono lifted his tear-stained face and gazed into his lover's eyes. Guilt was etched there. "The day after is always the worst you know that."

"I know but I hate to see you suffer."

"I know and I love you all the more for your concern but, it's what I want."

Atoni sighed and captured his lips. Their tongues twisted and danced for what seemed like an eternity. Hard cocks kissed each other.

"I have to get ready for work. Why don't you take another soothing bath?"

"I will after you leave but I'd like to have breakfast with you first." He moved away and pulled on his robe.

Atoni nodded.

"Cereal and toast?' Lono asked as he moved towards the door.

"Yes, please," Atoni said before heading back to the shower.

~*~

The smell of fresh coffee assailed Atoni's senses as he strode down the passageway and entered the kitchen.

Lono glanced around from where he was buttering toast and sighed. The man was drop dead gorgeous. Freshly showered and dressed in a dark blue suit with crisp white shirt and red tie, he was enough to start his mouthwatering.

"Stop looking at me like you want to eat me," Atoni growled as he reached for the coffee pot.

"Oh, but I do," Lono laughed.

He set the buttered toast on the table, alongside boxes of cereal, and both men sat down. Lono ensured the cushions on his chair were firmly in place before lowering himself gently.

"What are you doing today?" Atoni asked as he shook cereal into a bowl.

"Housework, washing, the usual. I thought I would make a pot roast for supper unless you would prefer something else."

"Pot roast sounds divine. Don't overdo things today. Give your ass a chance to recover."

"If I'm busy working, I won't be sitting on it."

"True but take it easy just the same."

"What have you got lined up today?" Lono asked.

"I have to type up witness statements and notes on the murder scene for the prosecution. Olina was formally identified by Molly yesterday and with Olina's recorded confession, I think the case is going to go through court pretty quick. The funeral for Nohea is today."

"So sad, such a waste. Do you mind if I slip out and purchase some gifts for the family today. Christmas is so close and, I thought as you have tomorrow off, we could go over and see the Okamu's."

"That sounds perfect. How about we have lunch at the hotel and go for a swim after we have been there?"

"I would love that, darling," Lono agreed.

Atoni stood. "Have to get going. I'll see you tonight."

He kissed Lono on the lips and let himself out.

Chapter Seven

Atoni lifted his head from the computer as Captain Akele Alepeleke, entered his office. He sprang to his feet. "Sir."

"Sit down." The Captain closed the office door and took the chair opposite Atoni.

"Do we have a problem, Sir?"

"I don't think so. How's the write up on the murder case coming along?"

"Almost done. I only have the Okamu's statement to complete and I'll send it over to Bill."

"Should be a quick case for Bill to prosecute but not easy sending a young woman to prison for most of her life."

"No, it's not. She's going to pay for a silly, thoughtless decision."

The Captain was silent for a few moments.

"Sir, is something on your mind?" Atoni's gut clenched. His stomach muscles knotted up. Dread washed over him. Instinctively he knew; his boss was going to ask if he was gay.

"For some time now, I have been hearing rumors about you and Corporal Kapule. I was hopeful you would trust me, and your colleagues, enough to come and discuss the matter with me."

In his mind, Atoni's world came crashing down. He slumped back in his chair. "Yes, the rumors are true, Sir. We are gay." He wasn't prepared to lie about it no matter what it cost. "I'm sorry, Sir. We didn't believe our personal life interfered with our work and decided it was no-one else's business. We suspected if it was out in the open, it would cost us our jobs and the respect of our colleagues."

"What the fuck are you talking about?"

"We believed some of our colleagues would refuse to work alongside us and you would refer us to the integrity board. We both assumed, if our relationship became known, it would be the end of our careers."

"Why?"

We've been in a relationship for three years. The police motto – Integrity, Respect and Fairness – probably isn't extended to us."

"Kinimaka, stop talking bullshit. You're one of the best, if not *the* best, Detective I have. Probably the best in the islands, if truth be known. I couldn't give a fuck if you're in a relationship with the man in the moon. I'm saddened that you felt the need to hide who you are from us, but more especially, your partner. I think he's about the only one who hadn't worked it out."

"What do you mean, Sir?"

"Roger had no idea until Ana questioned him about you and pointed out the fact you were gay. He came to see me this morning."

"Does he want another partner?" Atoni considered Roger a friend. He was devastated to think he would turn on him.

The Captain's eyes widened. "Of course not. He came to see me because he was concerned Ana might cause problems for you and Kapule. I've spoken with her, and advised her, there is no problem with anyone's sexual persuasion in this station."

"Thank you, Sir."

"No need to thank me. We have four other gay police walking the beat. We don't want any relationships openly flaunted, be they gay or otherwise, but we don't want you to fear your workplace colleagues either. I respect and appreciate your discretion and, I can assure you, the way you and Kapule are treated will not change."

"I hope not, Sir."

"It won't but in future, talk to me."

"I guess the truth is, we were scared," Atoni admitted.

"Don't be. We can work around almost anything." The Captain stood and Atoni pushed to his feet. "Finish your report and go home."

"Yes, Sir." Atoni watched as the Captain left his office and Roger appeared at the door.

"Atoni, can I come in?" he asked meekly.

Atoni sat down. "Of course, you can. Close the door and sit down."

Roger did as he'd been asked. "I'm sorry I went to the Captain but I was worried about you and Kapule when Ana told me."

"I understand but you could have come to me."

"I discussed what Ana said with Jenny last night, she urged me to take it straight to the Captain so there wouldn't be any trouble for you both. Jenny said she knew you were together but respected your rights to keep it private. Fuck, she didn't even tell me - *her* husband and *your* partner. You must think I'm pretty dumb not to have known."

Atoni laughed. "I wondered if you knew but Lono insisted, you had no idea. Didn't you wonder why I never talked about women?"

"Not until Ana talked to me. The pieces fell into place after that. You know it would never make any difference to me, don't you?"

"Even the closest of families come apart at the seams over something like this. I didn't want to risk losing yours and Jenny's friendship."

"You had nothing to worry about. I don't care if you live and sleep with a Martian. You're my partner and, I would like to believe, a very good friend."

Atoni laughed again.

"What?" Roger asked.

"According to the Captain, and now you, I can fuck the man in the moon and a Martian. You are a good friend and I appreciate your honesty. Thanks."

Roger stood. "I'm off home, Cap gave me the afternoon off. I'll see you in a couple of days."

"I have this report to finish and after I drop it off to Bill, I'm off home too."

A tear sprang to Atoni's eye as Roger left. His relief was enormous. He needed to get home to Lono and tell him the good news. He felt as if a ton weight had been lifted off his shoulders.

~*~

Atoni threw his keys on the hall table, kicked off his boots and strode to the kitchen. The room was empty. "Lono, where are you?" Silence. "Must be out shopping."

He helped himself to a bottle of water from the fridge before making his way to the bedroom. He was lulled off to sleep by the whirr of the overhead fan.

Lono whistled as he unlocked the door of the apartment and carried his purchases inside. He noticed Atoni's boots by the door and his keys on the table. A thrill ran down his spine, his lover was home early. He stiffened, a terrifying thought coming to mind. Had Ana spoken with the Captain? Were they both now unemployed?

Lono dumped the parcels on a bench in the kitchen and rushed to the bedroom. Atoni was sound asleep, naked and spread-eagled. Lono groaned with want and his dick leaped with interest. Stripping off his clothes, he crawled onto the bed and lowered his lips onto Atoni's.

Atoni responded immediately, his arms surrounded Lono's naked body and pulled him close. Their lips molded together, tongues twisted in their erotic dance. They separated, breathless.

"You're home early, darling. Is everything okay?" Lono asked.

"Everything is fabulous, sweetheart. The paperwork for the court case is finished and Cap said to take the afternoon off." Atoni smiled.

Lono became suspicious. "Why the cheeky, hiding something, smile?"

"The Captain came to my office today. He wanted to chat."

"Oh, no."

"Don't panic, sweetheart." Atoni placed a kiss on Lono's forehead and relayed the conversation which had taken place.

"So the Captain suspected all along about us being in a relationship?" Lono mused.

"Yes, he did. When I think about it, we have been pretty stupid. Cap is an ex-detective. Our colleagues are detectives and cops. With the exception of Roger, who can be as thick as molasses sometimes, it should have been obvious that they would know."

"Guess we're pretty thick too, huh?"

Atoni laughed. "Yeah, for smart men, we can be real stupid sometimes."

"I'm so glad everything has worked out. We have Ana to thank for not having to be scared anymore."

"Yes, we do. I'm pleased Roger went straight to Cap for advice, if he'd come to me, I would have tried to persuade him to keep it quiet. Nothing would have been resolved. By the way, we have been invited to Roger and Jenny's for Christmas lunch. I told him I would talk with you and give him a call."

"Our first invite as a couple. I would love to go, darling."

"I'll call him later. Right now, I want a nice slow fuck. How's the ass?"

"Sore but bearable. I had an oil bath after you left for work and rubbed lotion into it. It's uncomfortable to sit down but not painful like it was."

Atoni nodded in understanding. "Did you get the gifts for the Okamu family?"

"Yes. I think they will like what we have for them."

"I'm sure they will. You have excellent taste. Now enough talking, it's time to fuck." Atoni flipped Lono onto his back. "Spread your legs and arms."

While Lono did as he'd asked, Atoni rose to rummage in one of their drawers.

Lono was excited. His cock slapped against his belly in anticipation of what was to come.

Atoni climbed onto the bed, his ass level with Lono's head. He plunged his hardened cock into Lono's welcoming mouth. As he pushed in and out, his lover sucked and licked. Faster, deeper, the explosion fierce and satisfying.

Atoni felt like he'd been sucked into a vortex as ribbons of cum spasmed from him. Lono narrowed his lips, gripping, refusing to release his sensitive appendage. When he was sure he couldn't take one minute more, his freedom was granted. He collapsed onto the bed and finished descending.

Lono didn't move. He knew to stay put until Atoni recovered.

After what seemed like hours, Atoni popped onto his knees and lowered his head onto Lono's flaccid cock. He teased and tickled the tip, the dick hardened. Lono clung tight to the railings of the bedhead, his knuckles whitened. He groaned with arousal. "Darling, please take all of me."

Atoni sucked the length into his moist, willing mouth and fondled the tightening balls.

Lono moved his hips up and down, thrusting his rod further into Atoni's mouth. His ass cheeks clenched.

While one hand twisted and pinched at Lono's nipples, causing the areola to pebble and harden, the other pinched and fondled the rest of the writhing body, including the ball sack.

Lights burst behind Lono's closed eyelids, his cock pulsed with delight. He was airborne, the edge close. Atoni's tongue forced its way into the hole of his penis and over he went. He thrashed as cum spurted from his dick with such force, it was like a high pressure water hose.

Atoni refused to let up on the sucking and laving.

Lono felt like he would go mad. His body spasmed violently, he needed to come down, but Atoni was relentless. What was it about this man, that he could shoot him to the stars and keep him there?

His hands released the bedhead and tangled in Atoni's hair. He tried desperately to pull his cock from his lover's mouth. "Please, darling. Please...," another eruption built and burst forth. He screamed with pain and delight.

Atoni slowed, allowing Lono to float down. Both men were soaked in sweat and exhausted. They drifted to sleep, their bodies entwined.

Chapter Eight

Atoni pulled his car into the Okamu's driveway. The lover's slid from the car and lifted the beautifully wrapped parcels from the trunk of the car.

"These look gorgeous, sweetheart. You have done an excellent job of selecting the gifts and wrapping them," Atoni said.

"Thank you, darling. I hope they like what I have selected."

"I'm sure they will."

The men strode up the path. At the front door, Atoni moved the packages so he was able to rap at the door.

Mr. Okamu opened the door and a look of surprise graced his face when he recognized the men with their arms full of gifts.

"May we come in, Mr. Okamu?" Lono asked.

Mr. Okamu stood aside. "Of course, come in. Go through to the living room while I fetch Ka Pua and Leialoha." He disappeared along a hallway.

Lono and Atoni entered the home. Atoni pushed the door closed with his foot before they padded into the living room. The gifts were placed on the floor and the men sat.

"Misters," the little girl squealed as she ran into the room. She threw herself onto Atoni's lap, wrapped her arms around his neck and placed a kiss on his cheek.

Lono laughed at the display of affection from a child who didn't know them very well. Before he knew what was happening, he found the lively girl in his arms. She planted a wet kiss on his cheek before bouncing down onto the floor.

Mr. and Mrs. Okamu stood by the door watching their grandniece. Although they smiled, their eyes were full of sadness.

Leialoha stood facing the men with her hands on her hips. "Kanakaloka is visiting tonight. Auntie and Uncle said I've been a good girl so I'll get a present."

Lono glanced at Atoni and then at the Okamu's. The little girl's enthusiasm was delightful. He crooked his finger at her indicating for her to come closer. "Have you been *really* good?" Lono asked.

She turned towards her guardians and they both nodded. Turning back to Lono, she took his face in her tiny hands. "I've been *really, really* good."

Lono laughed and the others joined in. After a few moments he feigned a serious face. "Well, Mr. Atoni and I were told you were a very good, very special little girl so we have brought you some presents."

"For me?" Leialoha ran to her aunt and uncle. "Auntie, Uncle, Misters brought me presents."

Mr. and Mrs. Okamu moved into the room and sat down. "You must remember to say thank you." Mrs. Okamu said.

"I will," she assured before dashing back to Lono and Atoni.

Atoni handed her a present wrapped in red and white Santa paper and trimmed with red ribbon. "Thank you," she said softly.

Sitting on the floor, she ripped off the ribbons and paper. She threw them onto the floor behind her and gazed at the box in her hands. Springing to her feet, she dashed to her Aunt.

"Auntie, look. It's a dolly. Her dress is pretty." She thrust the box at her aunt who carefully removed it from the packaging and handed it back. "She's beautiful, thank you Misters." She hugged the doll to her chest and rocked it.

When Atoni glanced at the Okamu's, he noticed tears in their eyes.

"I have one for you too," Lono said. He held out another beautifully wrapped present.

Leialoha moved closer, placed the doll on the floor and accepted the gift. "Thank you," she said before sitting down next to the doll and tearing the ribbons and paper away.

"A pram. It's a dolly pram," she squealed with excitement.

Lono dropped to his knees and helped her pull it from the box. The doll was placed inside with great care.

The excitement continued as Leialoha opened parcels with a crib, high chair and bath set. The final present pushed her excitement over the top. The squeals were ear piercing as she tore away paper and revealed a small trike.

Lono and Atoni assembled the trike and, along with the Okamu's, they carried it and the child outside so she could begin riding. Leialoha pedaled up and down the street, laughing and squealing.

The adults watched closely.

"Thank you so much for the gifts and for bringing joy to Leialoha. You have a true Christmas spirit. You are both very kind," Mrs. Okamu said.

"It's our pleasure. We organized a collection for Leialoha and this is what we have so far." Lono handed a small passbook over. Mr. and Mrs. Okamu both gasped when they saw the balance was eight thousand dollars. "We have placed it into a college fund for her and we will add to it periodically."

"We have no words to thank you enough for this. Leialoha will have a good life but we are not wealthy people. This will help us a great deal. Your generosity will not be forgotten and we would be honored if you and your colleagues visited from time to time," Mr. Okamu said.

"We have a small gift for both of you but, we would like you to open it tomorrow if you don't mind. You have a beautiful little girl to raise and I know she will help you to overcome the sadness of losing your niece," Atoni said.

Mr. Okamu nodded sadly. "She is so much like her mother. We laid Nohea to rest yesterday. She is now with her Mama and Papa and I know she will watch over us while we raise her daughter to be as beautiful as she was."

Neighbors' children had joined Leialoha and were admiring her trike. Lono and Atoni watched as she pointed towards them and heard her say, "Misters buyed it for me. They buyed me a dolly and dolly things too."

"I think it's time we were going," Lono told the Okamu's. "I hope your Christmas isn't too sad. You will be in our thoughts."

The men shook hands and Mrs. Okamu placed a kiss on their cheeks.

"Again, thank you so very much. We are very grateful Nohea's murderer was brought to justice so quickly and we are thankful for Leialoha's gifts," Mr. Okamu said.

"Leialoha, come and say goodbye to Mr. Lono and Mr. Atoni," Mrs. Okamu shouted out.

The little girl came running, the trike pulled along behind. She flung herself into Lono's arms first. "Thank you." He was rewarded with another wet kiss. He handed her onto Atoni and she placed a kiss on his cheek before wriggling to get down. "Bye, misters," she called as she disappeared back to her friends.

Lono and Atoni climbed into the car. "Take care and we will drop by soon," Lono said.

Atoni fired up the engine and they headed for home.

"I think we helped cheer them a little. You did a terrific job, sweetheart. Her little eyes lit up when she saw the trike," Atoni said.

"It seems to be what most kids want these days."

"How did you know?"

"I watched children in the stores. I saw what they headed for and I figured Leialoha would want the same."

"You never cease to amaze me. Have I told you how very much I love you?"

"Not for the last half an hour," Lono laughed. He ran his hand over Atoni's thigh and smiled when he saw his cock leap. "I think you could show me when we get home."

"That sounds perfect to me. We have nothing else to do today. An afternoon in bed sounds wonderful."

"Hmmm, and a glass of good wine."

I can think of several ways to enjoy wine with you." Atoni grinned.

Lono slapped his thigh lightly. "Darling, you have a mischievous mind."

Atoni glanced at his thigh before sneaking a quick look at Lono.

"Oops." Lono was well aware he would pay for the slap. His dick danced with excitement. "I hope Mr. and Mrs. Okamu like the framed picture of their niece," he said in an attempt to distract Atoni.

"It was fortunate you were able to locate the picture on the internet and the filigree frame was beautiful. I'm sure it will take pride of place on their mantel." Atoni guided the car into the underground car park. "Now, we have business to settle."

The men held hands as they approached the lift to their apartment. Lono trembled with excitement.

About the Author

I'm an Australian author who writes in a variety of genres, including Western romance, historical romance, Gay Romance, and contemporary romance.

I have published over 60 books and novellas, many of which feature strong, independent heroines and rugged, alpha male heroes. Some of my popular series include the Outback Australia series and The Carter Brothers series.

My books are known for their well-researched historical details and vivid descriptions of the Australian landscape.

My work has garnered praise from readers and critics alike, and I have won several awards for my writing.

If you're interested in learning more about my books:

Linktree

https://linktr.ee/SusanHorsnell

Milton Keynes UK
Ingram Content Group UK Ltd.
UKHW020948221123
433051UK00020B/854